This book belongs to:

For Theo Ward and Nat Tan, *the Tuba Man*, with love.
K.S.

Sir Charlie Stinky Socks would like to donate 10% of the royalties from the sale of this book to Naomi House Children's Hospice.

EGMONT
We bring stories to life

First published in Great Britain 2012
by Egmont UK Limited
This edition published 2015
The Yellow Building, 1 Nicholas Road
London W11 4AN

www.egmont.co.uk

ISBN (PB) 978 1 4052 7772 3

A CIP catalogue record for this title
is available from the British Library

The Tale Of Two Treasures

Kristina Stephenson

EGMONT

Once upon a dusty shelf – in the musty space where a precious book should have been – the king of the castle (on top of the hill) found . . .

a paper scroll.

He unrolled it and found a

MYSTICAL MAP

showing the way to a world underground. There was

a **Tomb of Doom**,

a River of Riddles,

a **Mine of Much Despair** . . .

and *there*, in a **Puzzling Pit** . . .

. . . something beyond compare!

"**TREASURE!**" said the king of the castle.

"Then **somebody** needs to fetch it!

Isn't it right
that a **bold**,
brave knight
should go
on such a quest?"

Oh yes!

How fitting then that

Sir Charlie Stinky Socks

just happened to be in the castle,

along with his faithful, fearless cat, Envelope

and his good grey mare.

Three fine fellows,

steadfast and ready.

Well, *nearly* ready, that is.

For the horse needed shoes,

the cat couldn't choose what he ought to take with him

and bold, brave Sir Charlie

had a dent in his trusty sword.

Oh no!

"Send for the **blacksmith**!"
cried the king of the castle.
"This knight must be prepared!"

Slightly scared, the **blacksmith** bowed
before the king of the castle,

while behind him,

his daughter did
her best to show
her father's wares:

a hero's helmet,
a shimmering shield
and a hammer to mend a sword.

"I think we're ready!"
said Sir Charlie Stinky Socks.

And, map in hand, the eager band
set off in search of the TREASURE.

Clip clop, clip clop, tippity, tippity, toe.

The echo of footsteps followed the friends
and *someone* watched them go.

The **MYSTICAL MAP**
took the trusty trio
to a flight of
stony stairs.

A curtain of
cobwebs hung
at the top but
what was at
the bottom?

A frightful feeling filled the cat.
Terror took over the mare.

Only Sir Charlie Stinky Socks
would dare to find out.

He put on his helmet.
He grabbed his shield.

He drew his
trusty sword

and . . .

"Hang on a second!" he said to the others. "This is so unfair. Isn't it right that a *well-prepared* knight should offer to share his mettle?"

Sir Charlie gave the cat his **helmet** and the good grey mare his **shield**, before wielding his sword and leading them . . .

. . . into the **Tomb of Doom**!
Eeek!
It was a fearful room,
but they **had** to go through.

Trip trap trip trap – tippity, tippity, toe.

Eerie footsteps followed the three

and skeletons watched them . . .

Envelope squealed. The grey mare reeled. Would they be squashed to a pulp? Gulp!

"Fear not!" said Sir Charlie to his frightened friends, "for there's **always** a secret door."
And there, on the floor,
in a bundle of bones,
he spotted . . .

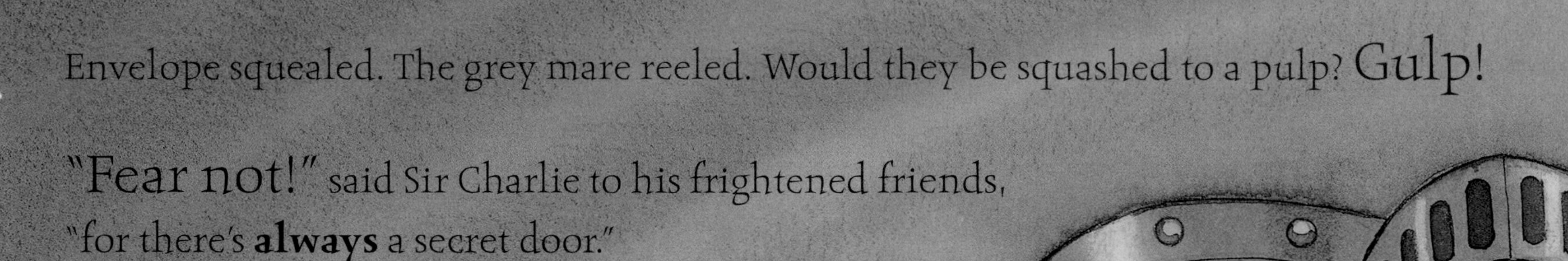

a skeleton key!

There **had** to be a lock to match but could Sir Charlie find it?

In less than a shake of a pussycat's tail, clever Sir Charlie did!

Phew!

A secret panel in the tomb slid open and . . .

. . . grow.

What?

Why did Sir Charlie and his steadfast friends suddenly seem to get bigger?

"Ye gads!" said the knight. "The walls are moving! The **Tomb of Doom** is . . .

. . . shrinking!"

. . . everyone leapt out!

Roots and shoots from the garden above spilled into the tunnel below, and foreboding footsteps followed the three as *someone* watched them go.

Pitter, patter, pitter, patter, down to the River of Riddles. Oh!

What a pity the **TREASURE** was on the *other* side!

Envelope didn't seem bothered. Nor did the *smug* grey mare.

It seemed the pair had found the solution quicker than Sir Charlie.

Ha!

Hip hop, clippety clop.

Wouldn't *this* be a doddle?

Nope!

The river rumbled.
The stepping stones crumbled and . . .

. . . the cat and the horse fell in.

Splash!

"Now *I'm* going to have to get wet!"

"Fiddlesticks!" said Sir Charlie Stinky Socks.

Splosh!

Sir Charlie
rescued his
faithful
friends
and pulled
them back
to the shore.

The **MYSTICAL MAP** was *soaked*.
But would you
believe it . . .

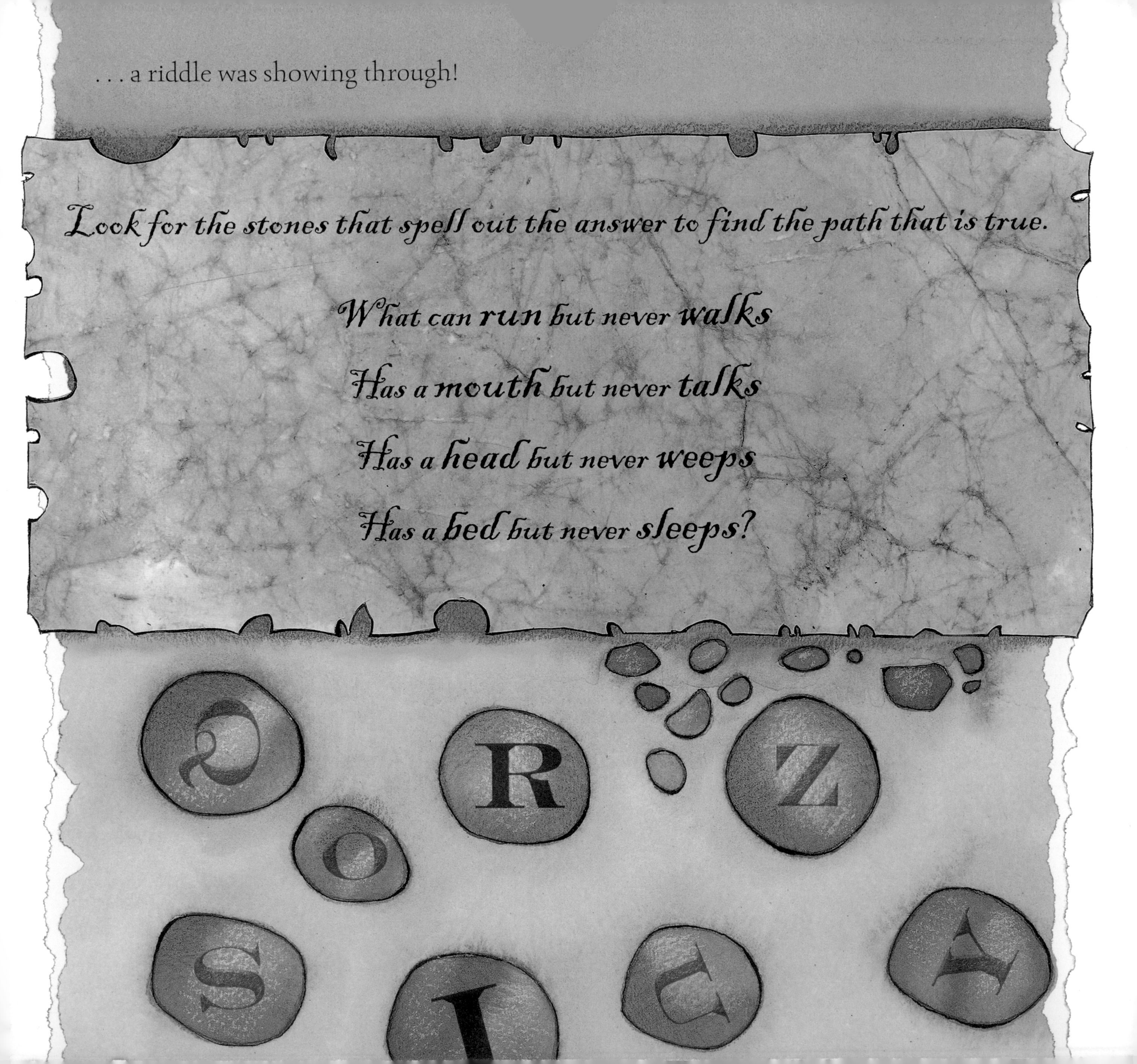
. . . a riddle was showing through!
Look for the stones that spell out the answer to find the path that is true.
What can run but never walks
Has a mouth but never talks
Has a head but never weeps
Has a bed but never sleeps?
Q
R
Z
O
S
I
U
A

One good guess and – yes!

Sir Charlie solved *this* puzzle too.

Hurrah!

Over the river but still dripping wet, Sir Charlie stopped to think.
"'Tis best we rest and dry ourselves beside a warming fire."
Drip, drip,
crackle, spit,
snore, snore, snore . . .

Clunk! Clunk!

What was that?

Envelope woke up.

Why was Sir Charlie dressed in his armour and *tiptoeing away?*

Wait for us! thought the puzzled cat and he rallied the groggy, grey mare.

They followed the knight, who followed the map to . . .

. . . the **Mine of Much Despair!**

Beware!

Envelope faltered. The grey mare froze.
The bold knight didn't flicker.
Quicker than you could say
'trusty sword' he . . .

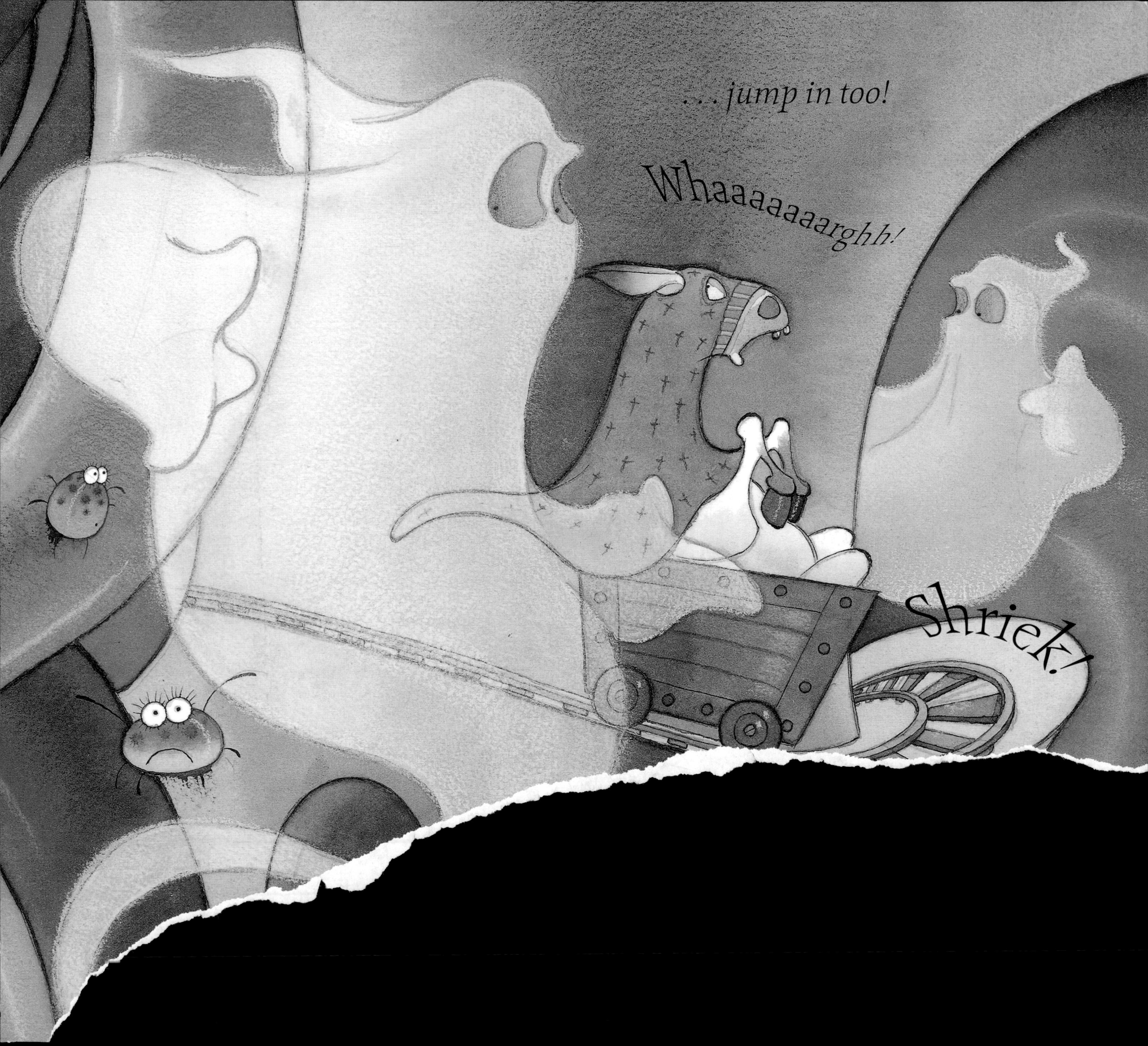
. . . jump in too!
Whhaaaaaaaarghh!
Shriek!

. . . you can guess
which chest it is in! Ha ha ha!"

"*Whoops!*" said the Goblie. "I nearly forgot!
There's a teensy-weensy catch.

To make things more
interesting . . .
why don't we say

you only get ***three*** *goes?*

Get it **right** and I promise the TREASURE is *yours*.
But get it *wrong* . . .

and ***I*** **get the cat and the horse.**"

Oh my!

But this was
Sir Charlie Stinky Socks.

He wouldn't need **three** goes!

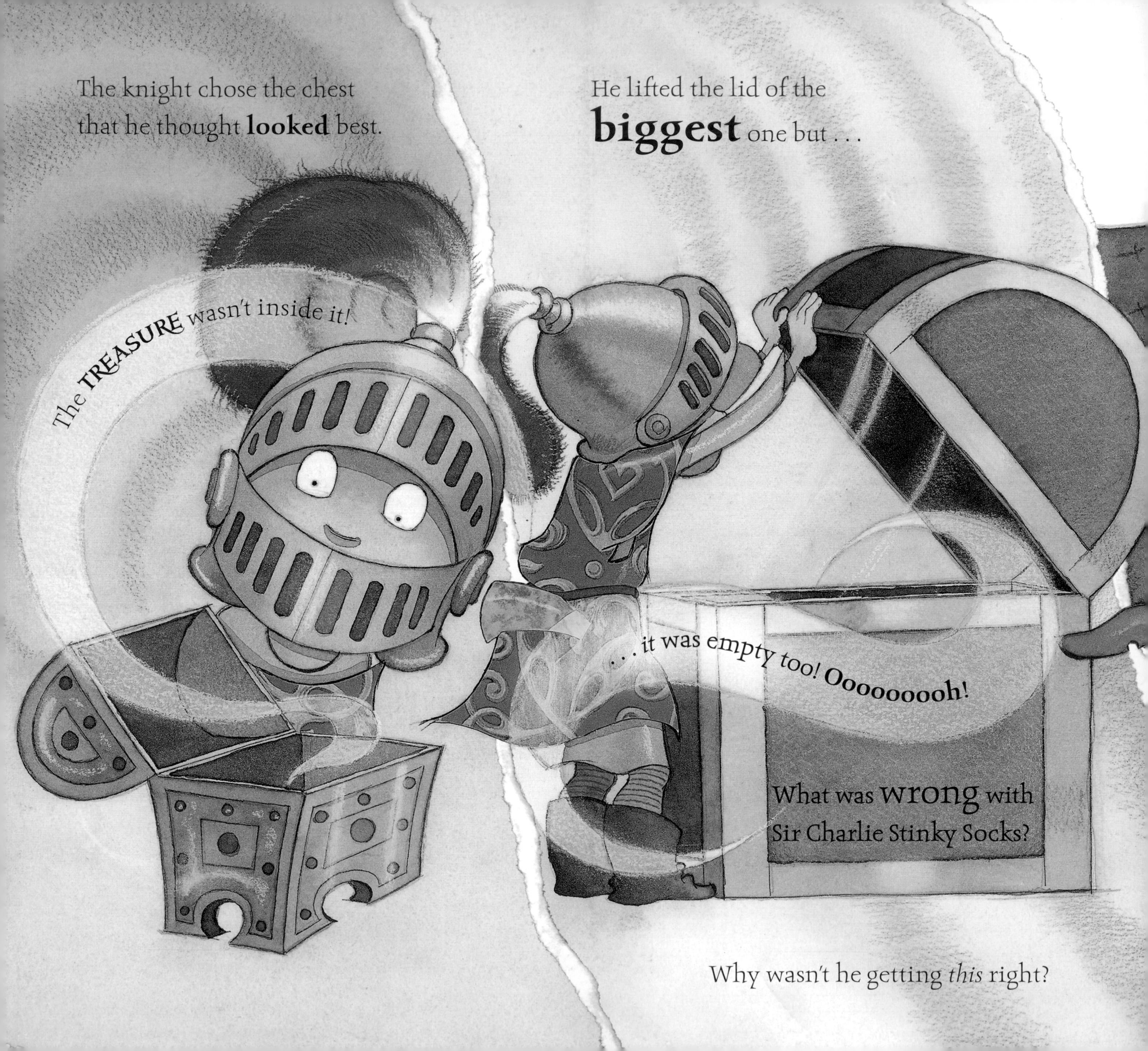

The knight chose the chest that he thought **looked** best.

The **TREASURE** wasn't inside it!

He lifted the lid of the **biggest** one but . . .

. . . it was empty too! **Oooooooh**!

What was **wrong** with Sir Charlie Stinky Socks?

Why wasn't he getting *this* right?

ir Charlie,

lmet?"

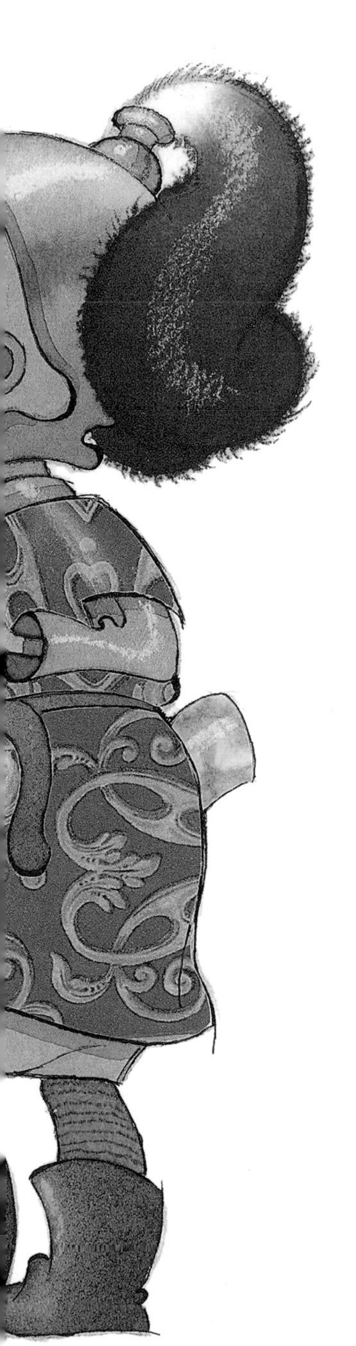

And come to think of it – since they sat down to rest at the River of Riddles – the knight *had been acting strangely*.

Could it possibly be that under that helmet . . .

Gasp!

. . . this wasn't Sir Charlie at all?

Trip trap,

trip trap,

tiptoeing into the light . . .

The blacksmith's daughter looked at Sir Charlie, tip tapping the **MYSTICAL MAP**.

"Oh! A knight would look at that," she said. "It's bound to give him a clue."

'Twas true!

X marked the spot on the **MYSTICAL MAP** and if she could find the *right* chest – not the biggest or the **best** but **the one that matched** –

then she'd find the **TREASURE**. Could you?

. . . the real knight,
Sir Charlie Stinky Socks,
appeared to save the day.

. . . there was the blacksmith's daughter!

"I'm sorry," she said to Sir Charlie. "I followed you from the castle an
by the River of Riddles, I borrowed your helmet and shield.

More than **anything else** in the w
I want to be . . .

. . . a knight."

The **Knobbly Goblie** was **mightily mad** because . . .

. . . the blacksmith's daughter did! Hooray!

Now all that was left was to find a way to get it to the king.

How fortunate then that the Puzzling Pit was down at the bottom of a well and – as luck would have it – Envelope the cat had chosen to bring a bow. **Ho ho**!

With one quick flick of his trusty sword, Sir Charlie made . . .

an arrow and *whizz, ping . . .* what a thing!

Everyone climbed out!

The king of the castle was overjoyed when he looked inside the chest and found the best kind of treasure for a fairy tale king . . .

. . . a fabulous Book of Spells!

Well, of course, he thanked Sir Charlie Stinky Socks, the cat and the good grey mare.

But he *knighted* the blacksmith's daughter and gave *her* . . .

a treasure
beyond
compare.